The Woman and th

A Folk Tale from Japan

Retold by Dawn McMillan

Illustrations by Xiangyi Mo and Jingwen Wang

Rigby®

A Harcourt Achieve Imprint

www.Rigby.com
1-800-531-5015

One cold winter day,

a little old woman went outside

to get some wood for her fire.

She saw a tiny bird by her door.

"Oh, little bird!" she said.

"You are so cold!

I will take you into my warm house."

3

The woman put the tiny bird
into a box by the fire and said,
"You will be hungry.
I will get you some food to eat."

The tiny bird did not eat the food.

It went to sleep in the box.

"Please don't die, little bird,"

said the woman.

"You are so beautiful!"

The woman put a cloth
over the box,
and then she went to bed.

In the morning,

the woman looked in the box.

She saw the tiny bird eating the food.

"Oh good!" said the woman.

"You are better today!"

The woman went outside
with the tiny bird.
"It's a warm day today," she said.
"Now you can fly away.
Off you go, little bird!"

But the tiny bird did not fly away.

It flew up into a tree

by the door

and sang in the morning sun.

From that day on,
the tiny bird sang and sang
to the little old woman.